Jill y las Habichuelas Mágicas

Jill and the Beanstalk

by Manju Gregory
illustrated by David Anstey

Spanish translation by Maria Helena Thomas

Jack, con su hermana Jill, subió por la colina.
Se cayó, se enfermó y ahora toma medicina.
No tiene qué comer, está muy agobiado,
porque el Gigante a su padre se ha tragado.

Jack climbed a hill with his sister Jill.
Jack fell down and now he's ill.
There's nothing to eat, they're feeling sad,
If only the Giant hadn't swallowed their dad.

Mamá le dice a Jill: "Si vas al mercadillo,
y vendes nuestra vaca, ¿habrá algún dinerillo?"

Mum asked Jill, "Do you think somehow
You could raise money selling our cow?"

Jill, al rato de camino, se encuentra con un hombre en la verja del vecino.
Dice él: "Mis habichuelas por la vaca a tu lado."
"¿Vaca por habichuelas? ¡Tú sí que estás chiflado!"
El hombre se lo explica: "Son mágicas, con ellas, serás rica."

Jill had barely walked a mile when she met a man beside a stile.
"Swap you these beans for that cow," he said.
"Beans!" cried Jill. "Are you off your head?"
The man explained, "these are magic beans. They bring you gifts you've never seen."

Jill a casa se las lleva y a mamá se las entrega.
"¡Si hubiera enviado a Jack!" -la madre ruega.
Y las arroja al suelo, pues no las quiere ver,
y la niña a la cama, sin nada de comer.

Jill took them home to show her mum
Who cried out loud, "I should have sent my son!"
She threw the beans down at Jill's feet
And sent her to bed with nothing to eat.

Al llegar la mañana, con el amanecer,
Jill encuentra una sorpresa, digna de ver.
Ha crecido una planta, trepadora, que ya llega hasta
el cielo, por ahora.
Sin perder un minuto ella empieza a subirse
y entre las hojas logra escabullirse.

Early to bed, early to rise,
Jill woke up at dawn with a mighty surprise.
A beanstalk had grown right up to the skies.
Catching hold of the stalk, clinging fast to the leaves,
She climbed the great plant as it swayed in the breeze.

Jill oye los gritos de su madre angustiada.
Y no los toma en cuenta, para nada.
Sigue subiendo, sin dejar de escalar,
porque a la misma cima quiere llegar.

Jill heard a shout, it was her mother!
"Come down at once, look after your brother!"
But Jill just kept on climbing, she didn't stop,
All the way upwards, right to the top.

Al llegar a la cima ve a una niña que llora:
"¿Dónde están mis ovejas?" -la niña implora.
"Se me han escapado mientras dormía hoy."
Y Jill le responde: "¿Pero yo dónde estoy?"

She leapt off the beanstalk, and heard a loud weep.
A little girl cried, "Oh, where are my sheep?
They've wandered away while I was asleep."
"Where am I?" asked Jill.

"Estás en la tierra donde vive el Gigante,
conocer tu intención es importante.
Si le quieres perdonar, vuelve a bajar.
Si buscas tu venganza, prepárate a luchar."

"You're in the land where the Giant lives.
Did you come to avenge or come to forgive?
With a wave of my crook now choose your fate,
Back down the beanstalk or onto the Giant's Gate?"

Jill se detiene frente al portón,
Temblando, eso sí, cual cobarde ratón.
Allí se encuentra una viejita, extraña,
quien del cielo limpia una tela de araña.
"¿Qué haces aquí, niñita?" -Pregunta la viejecita.

Jill stood in front of the Giant's house
Feeling tiny and scared like a quivering mouse.
A strange old woman was standing by,
Brushing cobwebs out of the sky.
"Little girl, why are you here? Why, oh why?"

Pero no hubo tiempo a replicar, porque la tierra se puso a temblar.
La viejecita, mirando a su entorno, dijo "¡corre muchacha, escóndete en el horno!
¡Sin respirar, sin suspirar, quédate quieta o te van a matar!"

As she spoke the ground began to shake, with a deafening sound like a mighty earthquake.
The woman said, "Quick run inside. There's only one place…in the oven you'll hide!
Take barely one breath, don't utter a sigh, stay silent as snow, if you don't want to die."

Jill, metida en el horno, sin saber qué habrá hecho, deseando estar en casa y en su lecho.
"Fi, fai, fo, fum" -el Gigante exclama- "¡Huelo sangre apetecible y humana!"
"Esposo, lo que hueles es pastel de avecilla, le he puesto veinticuatro, es una maravilla."

Jill crouched in the oven. What had she done? How she wished she were home with her mum.
The Giant spoke, "Fee, fi, faw, fum. I smell the blood of an earthly man."
"Husband, you smell only the birds I baked in a pie. All four and twenty dropped out of the sky."

El Gigante responde: "¡No me gusta ese plato!
¡Quiero algo que me quite el hambre por un buen rato!"
Y escondida en el horno, sin moverse de alli,
Jill ve como el Gigante devora un jabalí.

The Giant bawled, "I have no wish to even try your dainty dish.
Wife, I need to eat. Go to the kitchen and fetch me my meat!"
From a gap in the oven door, Jill watched the Giant devour a wild boar.

El Gigante no está, para nada, contento,
y grita "¡Trae mi ganso, no espero ni un momento!"
Y cerrando los ojos dice "¡GANSO, ADELANTE!"
Y el ganso pone un huevo, de oro deslumbrante.
Se divierte contanto, uno a uno
los huevos que tiene, de oro puro.
El gigante se duerme y comienza a roncar
como un león que ruge, repleto a reventar.

The Giant sat back, he wasn't happy.
He bellowed: "Get me my goose,
and make it snappy."
Saying, "Goose deliver," he closed his eyes.
It lay a bright golden egg,
much to Jill's surprise.
The Giant had a lot of fun,
Counting solid gold eggs one by one.
Then he fell asleep and started to snore
Sounding just like a mighty lion's roar!

Jill decide escapar mientras duerme el Gigante
y sale del horno muy sigilosamente.
Entonces recuerda a su amigo Tom pulgar
quien había robado un cerdo para cenar.
Cogiendo el ganso, corriendo y pensando
"A la trepadora de prisa y volando."

Jill knew she could escape while the Giant slept.
So carefully out of the oven she crept.
Then she remembered what her friend, Tom, had done.
Stole a pig and away he'd run.
Grabbing the goose, she ran and ran.
"I must get to that beanstalk as fast as I can."

Deslizándose por el tallo, gritando "¡He llegado!"
Salen Jack y su madre, ambos muy asustados.

She slid down the stalk shouting, "I'm back!"
And out of the house came mother and Jack.

"Tu hermano y yo nos hemos preocupado, pensando que algo malo habría pasado."
"No, mamá" -dice Jill- "he tenido un retraso y mira lo que llevo bajo el brazo."
Y repitiendo la orden de "¡GANSO, ADELANTE!"
Éste pone otro huevo, de oro deslumbrante.

"We've been worried sick, your brother and I. How could you climb that great stalk to the sky?"
"But Mum," Jill said, "I came to no harm. And look what I have under my arm."
"Goose deliver," Jill repeated the words that the Giant had said,
And the goose instantly laid a bright golden egg.

Así que la visita al Gigante en cuestión resuelve el hambre y la desesperación.

Jill's visit to the Giant's lair kept her family from hunger and despair.

Jack de su hermana se siente celoso
y quisiera haber sido el héroe valeroso.
Así repite a todos, con mucha certeza:
"¡Si hubiera sido yo, le corto la cabeza!"

Jack couldn't help feeling envious of his sister Jill.
He wished he'd climbed a beanstalk instead of a hill.
Jack boasted a lot and often said
If he'd met the Giant he would've chopped off his head.

Y a pesar de tenerlo tan prohibido
Jill, por la trepadora, una vez más ha subido.
Esta vez trepa bien, pero bien disfrazada,
y sube hasta el cielo, bastante cansada.

Their mother had warned them not to climb that stalk
But Jill was fed up with Jack's idle talk.
One day, in clever disguise, Jill climbed up the beanstalk
And reached the skies.

La viejita de entonces parece deprimida
y es que su marido le da muy mala vida.
La pobre no ha tenido ni un solo descans
desde que al Gigante le robaron el gans

The old woman sat by the gate looking sad,
The evil Giant treated her bad, very bad.
He'd become more gruesome by the day,
Since his goose had been stolen away.

La viejita a Jill no la reconoció pero los pasos del Gigante sí los oyó.
"¡Escóndete!" –grita. "Pues viene con hambre y te comerá si huele tu sangre."

The Giant's wife didn't recognise Jill,
But she heard the sound of thundering footsteps coming down the hill.
"The Giant!" she cried. "If he smells your blood now, he's sure to kill."

"Tic, tac, toc.
¡Escóndete en el reloj!"

"Hickory dickory dock,
Quick, go hide in the clock!"

"Fi, fai, fo, fum" -el Gigante exclama-
"¡Huelo sangre apetecible y humana! ¡Y le voy a cortar la cabeza!"
"Lo que hueles son tartas que acabo de hornear,
usé la receta de nunca acabar."
"Yo soy el Gigante, quiero carne roja, vete a la cocina
y trae lo que se me antoja."

"Fe fi faw fum, I smell the blood of an earthly man.
Let him be alive or let him be dead, I'll chop off his head," the Giant said.
"You smell only my freshly baked tarts, I borrowed a recipe from the Queen of Hearts."
"I'm a Giant, wife, I need to eat. Go to the kitchen and get me my meat."

El Gigante, como siempre, la devora
y más carne pide al cabo de una hora.
Y después solicita a su señora esposa
que traiga el arpa de oro maravillosa.
El Gigante dice: "¡MÚSICA!" -se siente aburrido.
Y el arpa produce un dulce sonido.

The Giant gorged on beast as before.
One full hour passed by, then he called for more.
His wife brought in a harp, the most magnificent of things,
Made out of pure gold with a hundred strings.
The Giant yelled: "Play," he was feeling bored.
The harp instantly played of its own accord.

Es como una nana suave y absorbente que duerme al Gigante instantáneamente.
Jill quiere ese arpa, la quiere bastante. Ya que toca sola y es fascinante.
Sale del reloj, coge el instrumento y sale corriendo sin perder ni un momento.

A lullaby so calm and sweet, the lumbering Giant fell fast asleep.
Jill wanted the harp that played without touch. She wanted it so very much!
Out of the clock she nervously crept, and grabbed the harp of gold whilst the Giant slept.

Va corriendo hacia la trepadora, tropieza con un perro y no se atora
cuando el arpa grita "¡MI DUEÑO, MI DUEÑO!"
Se despierta el Gigante de un profundo sueño Jill corre de prisa y sigu en su empeño.

To the beanstalk Jill was bound, tripping over a dog, running round and round.
When the harp cried out: "MASTER! MASTER!" The Giant awoke, got up and ran after.
Jill knew she would have to run faster and faster.

El Gigante chilla: "¿Crees que escaparás?
¡Yo quiero mi arpa y me la darás!"
Abrazada al arpa, Jill sigue escapando
"Mejor que me vaya de prisa y corriendo."

The Giant howled, "So you think you can run!
Look what happened to Tom, the piper's son!"
Holding onto the harp, Jill ran and ran,
"I must get to that beanstalk as fast as I can."

Llegó a la trepadora y se deslizó, mientras que el arpa
repite "¡MI DUEÑO!"
El Gigante, corriendo tras ella siguió, y por menos de
nada logra su diseño.
Pero Jill llegó abajo y cogió un buen hacha
y cortó la planta, la lista muchacha.

She slid down the stalk, the harp cried: "MASTER!"
The great ugly Giant came thundering after.
Jill grabbed the axe for cutting wood
And hacked down the beanstalk as fast as she could.

Cada paso del gigante causaba un temblor y Jill dio un gran hachazo con fuerza de horror.
Ante el gran asombro de Jack, Jill y su madre, se cayó el Gigante…
Y era tal su peso, y estaba tan alto, que excavó su tumba, del impacto.

Each Giant's step caused the stalk to rumble. Jill's hack of the axe caused the Giant to tumble.
Down down the Giant plunged!
Jack, Jill and mum watched in wonder, as the giant CRASHED, ten feet under.

Mamá, Jack y Jill ahora viven cantando
al son de la música del arpa sonando.

Jack, Jill and their mother now spend their days,
Singing songs and rhymes that the golden harp plays.

Text copyright © 2004 Manju Gregory
Illustrations copyright © 2004 David Anstey
Dual language copyright © 2004 Mantra
All rights reserved

British Library Cataloguing-in-Publication Data:
a catalogue record for this book is available
from the British Library.

First published 2004 by Mantra
5 Alexandra Grove, London N12 8NU, UK
www.mantralingua.com